Doggy Tales

Bedtime Stories for Dogs

BEVERLEY CONRAD

Pictures by Joel Schick

A DELTA BOOK

A DELTA BOOK
Published by Dell Publishing Co., Inc.
1 Dag Hammarskjold Plaza
New York, New York 10017

The stories "Cinderdoggy," "Snowdoggy and the Seven Chihuahuas,"
"The Story of Little Red Riding Dog," "Rumpleddogskin," and
"Jack and the Bonestalk" first appeared in *Dogtales* by Beverley Conrad,
published in 1978.

Delta ® TM 755118, Dell Publishing Co., Inc.
Printed in the United States of America
First printing — January 1980

Library of Congress Cataloging in Publication Data

Conrad, Beverley, 1950–
Doggy tales.

(A Delta book)
1. Dogs—Anecdotes, facetiae, satire, etc.
I. Title.
PN6231.D68C6   813'.54   79-25417

ISBN: 0-440-52132-7

Dedicated to Maggy May

my loyal little adopted companion from the animal shelter. whose constant scratching kept me awake nights long enough to tell stories to get her to sleep.

TABLE OF CONTENTS

Introduction

Doggy Tales is specially designed to be read aloud by the masters and mistresses of the world to their dogs.

It is a simply written and constructed book, chock full of pictures and philosophies relevant to a dog's life.

Doggy Tales is for the novice dog-tale spinner. It is a beginner's book in the art of educating a dog through good literature. It is for the person who enjoys talking to his dog, but occasionally runs out of things to say. And it is for the semiliterate dog who may have found Dick and Jane bland, but really got off on Spot.

When reading this book to your dog, we suggest that you let the dog sit right next to you, on the furniture, if necessary, so that he can look at the pictures. Read with emotion. In order to convey this, of course, you will have to employ the use of some simple sound effects — an occasional bark, a whine, a growl.

As your dog becomes acquainted with each tale, he may beg you to act out his favorites with him. This is not difficult. We suggest that you start with a simple perking of the ears. Tail-wagging will come with time.

As you lead your dog through the world of *Doggy Tales*, you will find that it will comfort, console, and soothe him. It will distract him from the noisy outside world and eliminate sudden barking attacks.

As he learns to read these for himself, you will find that he will no longer be interested in the garbage or yesterday's newspaper. He will only be interested in the meaty stories of *Doggy Tales.*

Settle back. Relax. Begin reading. And if your pet dogears his favorite pages, pay no attention. He's only following his natural instinct.

Cinderdoggy

NCE UPON A TIME there lived a beautiful little doggy named Cinderdoggy. She was a kind and gentle doggy with a good disposition. She was also good with children.

Poor Cinderdoggy, however.

She was but a poor, mangy mongrel, and because she got lost sometime during her puppyhood, she was forced to live in a house with three mean stepdogs. Poor Cinderdoggy had to work all day, picking up after these mean stepdogs. When they got into the garbage, she was blamed. When they chewed up shoes, she was blamed. And when their mistress got fleas, she got the flea bath.

One day a notice was put up at dogfood counters around the countryside that said there would soon be a ball.

Prince, a handsome dog in the area with fine breeding and lots of papers, was looking for a mate. Soon he would have a gala affair held at his dogcastle, and there he would choose the loveliest dog as his mate.

Poor Cinderdoggy had to help her stepdoggies dress for the ball. She brushed their coats, shined their collars, and trimmed their toenails. After they left, she whined. She was very sad.

Lo and behold, all of a sudden what should appear in midair but a strange little doggy with wings. At first Cinderdoggy was afraid. Then she barked.

"Do not be afraid and bark," the strange little dog said. "I am your fairy goddog. I have come so that you too can go to the ball."

"But I can't go," Cinderdoggy said. "I have nothing to wear. They took all the best collars. I have nothing but this old shoe," she said, looking down.

15

"Fetch the shoe!" said the flying dog. So Cinderdoggy did and at once the old shoe became a beautiful rhinestone collar, the kind rich dogs wear.

"Fetch the bone!" the strange flying dog said. And at once the dogbone became a car for Cinderdoggy to go for a ride in.

Then POOF! All at once Cinderdoggy became sleek and beautiful, and on her paws appeared four tiny glass shoes.

"But you must not stay out all night," the fairy god-dog cautioned. "At midnight my magic wears off, and you will once again become poor Cinderdoggy."

Well, I'll tell you, Prince saw Cinderdoggy and immediately fell in love with her. At the ball they danced together as dogs do, and before Cinderdoggy knew it, the evening was over.

As the clock struck midnight Cinderdoggy leaped into the air and hightailed it down the stairs. On the way down she lost one of her tiny glass shoes.

Prince, of course, noticed this and knew he would

begin searching for the beautiful owner of this shoe at once.

"It shouldn't be hard to find her," he said. "I'll just look for a dog wearing only three slippers."

Sure enough, the following morning when Prince was out taking his walk, he saw Cinderdoggy picking up some trash that her three stepdogs had thrown around the night before. And lo! he noticed that Cinderdoggy had on only three glass shoes.

Cinderdoggy and Prince began wagging their tails so much that Cinderdoggy could hardly sit when Prince told her to sit. But when he said "Give me your paw," she did, and on it he put the tiny glass shoe. It was obviously hers.

Prince and Cinderdoggy lived happily ever after, while the stepdoggies took off for greener pastures.

Cinderdoggy could hardly believe her good fortune.

Snowdoggy and the Seven Chihuahuas

NCE UPON A TIME in a far-off country, there lived a beautiful and kind dog named Snowdoggy. She was named this because she was part Siberian husky.

Nearby, in a huge kennel that could resemble a castle if the light was right, lived the ruler of the country. Her name was Queenie.

19

Queenie was a very vain dog, probably because she was queen of all the dogs, but more likely because she had a magic mirror that told her every day that she was the most beautiful dog in the world.

Each day Queenie would go to the mirror and ask, "Mirror, mirror on the doghouse wall, who's the prettiest dog of them all?" and the mirror would answer, "You."

One day, however, Queenie asked the mirror this question and although Queenie had just had a flea bath and had been clipped and groomed and really looked pretty good for the dog that she was, the mirror answered, "Sorry, Queenie, but Snowdoggy just had a bubble bath too, and actually looks better than you."

Well, I won't even use the word to describe Queenie's attitude after hearing that! Let it suffice to say that she became a rather "touchy" female dog.

"Fetch Snowdoggy!" she told her guard dogs. "And banish her from this kennel!"

The guard dogs found Snowdoggy just going about the business of being a dog, someplace in the vicinity of the grand doghouse. They told her what Queenie had said. Alas, poor Snowdoggy. What could she do but pack up her belongings — her dish, her collar, her dogbone — and leave.

Poor, poor Snowdoggy! It was the longest walk *she* ever took.

After many miles, she chanced upon a tiny doghouse in the woods. Outside the door she saw seven little bowls filled with water, and since she was very thirsty, she decided to lap some of it up.

Soon she heard a strange sound, the sound dogs would make if they tried to whistle. Turning around quickly, what did she see but seven little chihuahuas.

After acquainting themselves with one another, in the way only dogs can do, they all began wagging their tails and walking in circles. The tiny dogs liked Snowdoggy and asked her to stay with them.

However, back at the dogcastle, Queenie thought she had successfully rid herself of any competition, and once again sat in front of the mirror and barked, "Speak!" Once again, though, the mirror answered, "You have sent Snowdoggy from the kingdom, Queenie, but she is still the most beautiful dog that lives. What with her coat as white as snow, her nose of blackest ebony, her —"

"Oh, shut up!" barked Queenie, and she set about finding a way to do Snowdoggy in.

Needless to say, it did not take her long to think of a way to do it.

She poisoned a luscious looking dogbone and went to find Snowdoggy, which wasn't a hard task — she just followed the trail Snowdoggy had left in the woods.

Being a fool for a good bone, Snowdoggy immediately accepted the meaty bone from Queenie, who had successfully disguised herself as a mangy old mutt. No sooner did she taste it than she lay down, rolled over, and fell into a deep sleep.

Of course the seven chihuahuas were most upset when they saw their friend and set about whining and howling.

Soon a young male dog known as Prince heard the racket and went to find out what it could be. Upon seeing Snowdoggy, he fell head over heels in love with her and he planted a kiss on the end of her nose!

Snowdoggy awoke and at once fell in love with the Prince.

They now live someplace in Boston.

Queenie is currently undergoing surgery for a snout-lift.

The Story of Little Red Riding Dog

 NCE UPON A TIME in a faraway wooded land, there lived a little doggy named Little Red Riding Dog. She was named this because one year for Christmas a well-meaning friend gave her a hooded red cape so that her ears wouldn't freeze.

One day Little Red Riding Dog's mother said, "Fetch the basket and fetch the bone and take them to your grandma's house."

Little Red Riding Dog leaped into the air. She was so happy that she was being allowed out of the house without her leash. Fetching the basket in her teeth, she took off down the wooded trail.

Soon she spied a little boy playing in the woods.

"You had better watch out, Little Red Riding Dog," the little boy said. "You don't have your leash on, and the dogcatcher is out today."

Little Red Riding Dog whined, then she hurried down the trail so that if the dogcatcher were around, he would not see her and certainly would not catch her.

Before long she was at her grandma's house, and when she scratched on the door, she heard a voice say, "Come in, Little Red Riding Dog," so she went in.

"Hello, Grandma," Little Red Riding Dog barked. "I fetched a bone for you from Mother's house."

"Fetch it here, my little granddog."

But Little Red Riding Dog's fur went up because it did not sound like her grandma anymore.

"Arf!" barked Little Red Riding Dog. "Grandma, what strange eyes you have!"

"The better to see you with."

"Grandma, what strange ears you have!"

"The better to hear you with."

"Grandma, what strange *paws* you have!"

"The better to catch you with!" And all of a sudden her grandma leaped from the bed, and all of a sudden it wasn't her grandma at all. It was the dogcatcher!

Little Red Riding Dog quickly leaped out of the window, and who should be standing there but the little boy. He promptly snapped a leash on her and was calmly walking her home by the time the dog-catcher saw her.

Before long she was safely inside her house and living happily ever after. And to this day, although she still likes going for walks without her leash, she certainly knows why it is better to wear one.

Rumpleddogskin

NCE UPON A TIME there lived a beautiful doggy named Lady who made the mistake of saying one day in conversation that she could spin straw into rawhide strips.

Immediately word spread, and before long King heard of this and summoned her to his dogcastle.

"I have heard of your ability to spin straw into rawhide strips," King said to Lady. "And I have decided to see if this is true. Tonight you will sit in a kennel and we will bring you straw. If it is rawhide strips in the morning, I will marry you. If it is not, I will send you to the pound." King was not known for being flowery and romantic. He was known for being blunt.

Lady did not know what to do. She couldn't really spin straw into rawhide strips — she couldn't even spin. She was bored the day she said that she could. When her master had told her to "speak," she decided to say something interesting for a change.

Poor, poor Lady. Here she was — in the doghouse and surely on her way to the pound. She whimpered.

Suddenly before her sat a strange dog with loose, hanging skin that fell in great folds around him.

"Don't cry, Lady," he said. "I will spin the straw into rawhide strips for you under one condition . . ."

"Anything, anything!" Lady barked, quietly of course, as she did not want King to think she was barking to herself.

"You must give me your firstborn litter."

That sounded fair to Lady. She was a young doggy
and did not, as yet, know what a litter was.

Without another "arf," the dog with the funny-
looking coat sat and quickly began spinning the straw
into delicious, chewy rawhide strips.

The next day King saw this, and before you could
blink an eye, he married Lady. She did not change her
name to Queenie, however, because she would only
answer to Lady.

Nine weeks to the day later Lady had a litter of
fifteen puppies. Lady had long since forgotten what

31

the strange dog had said to her. She was too busy realizing what a litter was.

One day as she was taking a break from her basket, the strange dog once again appeared before her. "Lady, I have come to take your litter," he barked, not half as friendly as before.

Lady's fur bristled. The strange dog should have known not to come so close to a lady dog with fifteen puppies.

He was not afraid. "But you promised!" he howled. And indeed Lady had promised. And she knew it.

She cried and whimpered and howled. She lay down, rolled over, and cried some more. In short she made a spectacle of herself.

The strange dog, sensing that she might be upset about losing her litter, decided to give her a chance. "Oh, all right," he said. "If you can guess my name in three days, you can keep your litter. If not...." And he was gone.

Lady began going through her *Names for New*

Dogs books that she had gotten after finding out what a litter was. But nowhere in the books could she find anything that even came close to the strange dog's name.

On the third day she decided to clean out her basket and set to dragging the old blanket into the sun to air. As she lay sunning herself she kept opening her eyes to look at the old blanket.

"That looks like someone I know," she mused to one of her maid dogs.

"It looks like an old rumpled dog skin to me," said the maid dog.

"That's it!" barked Lady and leaped into the air over and over, once again making a spectacle of herself.

A loud howl was heard someplace outside the dogcastle wall, and Lady knew that she was right.

Rumpleddogskin left the country, which was too bad, for eight weeks later a sign was hung outside the dogcastle wall that read

PUPPIES — MIXED BREED — FREE.   INQUIRE WITHIN.

Jack and the Bonestalk

 NCE UPON A TIME, in a country that is neither here nor there, lived a little dog named Jack. Granted, it was a strange name for a dog, but Jack's mother thought that it suited him.

One day Jack's mother barked to him, saying, "Jack, come here! We're starving to death! I need you to go find a dogbone!" Jack's mother could be very dramatic, but generally she barked the truth.

Jack, who was busy sniffing at the lawn, looked up and saw his mother holding an old tennis shoe.

"Here, Jack," she said. "Take this old tennis shoe to the butcher and ask him for an old hambone. We cannot get anything more out of this sneaker, but a hambone would do us well."

Jack was a well-trained dog, having been to dog obedience school once, so he set out for the butcher shop directly.

Well, once the butcher saw the old tennis shoe, he naturally wanted it in trade. It matched one he already had. The butcher, who did not like the condition in which his tennis shoe was returned, slyly said to Jack, "Here, take this rubber dogbone and go bury it. Soon it will grow into a tall stalk and dogbones will grow on it forever."

Jack, again, being an obedient dog, did as he was told.

When Jack got home, he told his mother what had happened.

"What?" she barked. "What am I to do with you, Jack, for doing such a foolish thing? Everyone knows bones don't grow on trees—let alone stalks! You just wait till your father gets home!" But she knew his father came home only once every six months and it would be a while before that. "We will surely starve to death!" she howled.

Jack felt bad at having disappointed his mother, and he went out and lay down near the spot where he had buried the rubber dogbone.

Lo and behold, the following morning as Jack sniffed about the lawn as usual, he accidentally watered the spot where he had buried the dogbone. Immediately the butcher's words came true.

And just as immediately Jack, who was not used to climbing trees or stalks, climbed it anyway.

At the top of the stalk Jack saw a large, foreboding doghouse. A BEWARE OF DOG sign hung on the gate.

Soon a growl was heard: "Fe-Fi-Fo-Fog. I smell the smell of an English dog."

Following the growl, Jack saw a rather large dog the size of three hundred Great Danes put together.

Jack, who was smart as well as obedient, believed in only picking on dogs his size and decided not to pick on this one.

He headed right back to the stalk, and down he climbed, not even bothering to gather dogbones on the way. And down the great giant dog followed, growling and licking his chops the whole way.

When he reached the ground, Jack did not have time to explain to his mother why he was chewing at the stalk and not the dogbones.

The stalk fell with a tremendous crash, and Jack breathed a sigh of relief. The great giant dog, Jack figured, had landed somewhere in Buffalo, many miles away.

Jack never did bother to explain to his mother why he preferred stalks to bones that day. His mother just figured that he was going through a stage — a famous vet had called it puperty.

Goldydog and the Three Bigger Dogs

NCE UPON A TIME in a land that will not be found on a road map, lived a beautiful little dog with the good fortune to have a coat of a multitude of long golden curls. Naturally she was named Goldydog.

One day little Goldydog was out for her morning walk and, in keeping with her adventurous nature, strayed off into a nearby woodland. Sniffing and prancing, prancing and sniffing, away she went, hardly aware that she was getting thoroughly lost.

All of a sudden what should she hear but a tremendous growl that all but frightened her out of her coat! She was relieved to find out that it was just her hungry stomach, but at the same time she also discovered that she was lost.

Alas and alack! Whimpering softly to herself, poor Goldydog tried in vain to find her trail, but since there had been neither rhyme nor reason to her prancing and sniffing, she could not. She howled.

Soon she spied a house in the woods. She was so happy, woofs cannot express it!

Racing up to the front door, she barked loudly, hoping to arouse the attention of whoever lived inside. No one answered. She scratched on the door of the house. Still no answer. Poor Goldydog did not know what to do. She had spent so much time being adventurous in the woods that she was now sleepy as well as lost and hungry. If only she could go lie down for just a little while.

She scratched one last time as loud as she possibly could, and the door, which was not locked at all, flew open! Goldydog's ears flew up! The fur on her back bristled.

Surely this was no average house. It did not smell of people or small dogs. *Au contraire!* It smelled strongly like the huge doghouse in her neighborhood — a place where no dog in her right mind would ever enter.

Goldydog perked up her ears and listened. Clearly whoever lived there was not at home. Happily wagging her tail, she went inside and sniffed the place over.

Prancing and sniffing, sniffing and prancing, feeling wild, free, and once again curious and adventurous, what should she chance upon but three huge dogdishes, each filled to the brim with savory delights.

"BowWOW!" she barked and licked her chops.

In the first bowl was a gigantic meaty dogbone. In

vain she struggled to drag the bone out of the dish.

In the second bowl was a huge mound of the most delicious gristle she had ever had the chance to sniff. But alas, it was too tough for her dainty little teeth to chew.

In the third bowl was an enormous pile of the most expensive dogfood she had ever seen — the kind her master needed a coupon to afford. Diving into it, as was her nature, she quickly ate the whole thing, though it was three times bigger than she.

Needless to say little Goldydog wanted to flop right down and sleep after her big meal, so she started to look for a place to curl up.

"What fun!" she barked, tossing caution to the wind. "No one at home and a whole houseful of furniture to get up on!" And what greeted her as she bounced into the living room but three giant overstuffed chairs.

So she tried the first one. Poor Goldydog. She was unable to jump up on it, as it was as overstuffed as she.

Then she tried the second one. It was a color called

Autumn Haze, however, and clashed with her coat. She sniffed at it, but did **not** bother to climb onto it.

Lo! What should she see but a third overstuffed chair. And this one suited her just fine. On it she climbed, and upon it she slept.

All of a sudden she heard a rattle and a crash, and the door to the house banged open! She heard the sound of a dozen dogpaws slapping the floor and she became afraid.

What was she to do? Here she was, obviously stuffed in an overstuffed chair that was certainly not hers, and here came twelve huge dogpaws with three huge dogs attached ready to get her!

"WOOF! Who's been smacking at my dogbone?" a very loud growl growled.

"WOOF! WOOF! Who's been nibbling at my gristle?" a louder growl growled.

"WOOF! WOOF! WOOF! Who's obviously been diving into my expensive dogfood?" an amazingly loud growl growled. "And ate it ALL up? That's impossible!"

The dozen dogpaws tramped into the living room, where Goldydog cowered deeper into the chair. Whatever would she do? Goldydog whimpered, "If I can only escape from these three bigger dogs, I vow I will never ever toss caution to the winds again."

"Who's been trying to climb my chair?" the first huge dog growled.

"Who's been sniffing at *my* chair?" the second huge dog growled.

"Who's been favoring *my* chair and obviously is currently taking a nap on it?" the third huge dog growled.

And then a great slapping and a-scrambling was heard as the three bigger dogs set after poor Goldydog. Poor little Goldydog just about lost all the curl in her pretty golden coat, she was so scared.

But as scared as she was, she was quick. Spying an open ground-floor window, she leaped out, never again to be tracked by the three bigger dogs. The open ground-floor window, you see, was only big enough for one doggy, and since all three had it in for her, all three bigger dogs tried to get through at once.

To this day Goldydog is living happily ever after. And to this day the three bigger dogs are still trying to get through the window!

The Story of Sleeping Doggy

NCE UPON A TIME, in a place where dogs congregate, lived a mother dog, a father dog, and a neat little puppy dog without a name. Fairly soon, as was the custom in that area, came the time that the puppy dog was to be licensed, for she was nigh six months old.

A great celebration was planned for that day because the puppy dog would also be named at that time. Invitations went out hither and yon, to every dog for blocks and blocks around — save one. The one who was not invited, you see, had a bad disposition and liked to pick dogfights for no particular reason. In short, she was a witch.

On the day of the great celebration when all the dogs were assembled in and about the great yard, the mother dog and the father dog stood and told the other dogs to sit.

"We have decided to name our puppy dog Doggy," barked the father dog, "because that is what she is." And around the neck of the puppy dog was placed a new leather collar and a shiny aluminum dog license.

"You may now fetch your gifts forward," added the mother dog.

Soon, all about the dogbed lay an enormous array of gifts — rawhide bones, colored rubber balls, ratty old shoes, and bars of sweet-smelling flea soap — all for little Doggy.

All of a sudden a great growl was heard. And who

should come racing in but the mean old dog who had not been invited!

"I have a gift for little Doggy," she growled. "Henceforth the only trick she will be able to do is *lie down!*" And with that she was gone.

At that pronouncement the pack of dogs began whimpering and whining until a certain little dog found its way to the front and said this:

"Little Doggy needn't worry. Eventually there will come a handsome dog named King who will kiss her and save her. It may take a while for him to get here, however, for he is from another neighborhood, if not another zoning district altogether." With that, she was gone.

As the months passed, it became evident that the mean old dog's curse had worked. Poor Doggy. Someone would say "Sit," and she would lie down. Someone would say "Shake hands," and she would lie down. Someone even tried to fool her into doing a different trick by saying "lie down." She lay down. She *always* lay down. Eventually some rather observant dogs in the neighborhood began calling her Sleeping Doggy, because *that* was what she was.

Eventually, along came the time for Sleeping Doggy to find a mate and settle down with a doghouse and puppies of her own. Woe to Sleeping Doggy, however. What dog in his right mind would have her?

Her mother dog and father dog fretted and whined. No dog they knew would court her. When dogs came to visit, she would not sit and shake hands and speak politely as refined doggies do. She would just lie down. Poor Sleeping Doggy could not even "beg" them to stay. Lying down was her whole act.

One day barks spread rapidly around the neighborhood, reporting that a strange dog had been sighted just hanging around. He had come from miles away and was quite obviously in search of something. How was he to know that he was the dog destined to dissolve the strange curse?

Following his nose — for what else could he do unless he walked backward — he found his way to the great yard of Sleeping Doggy.

Lo! She was the most beautiful dog he had ever seen! He did not even notice the huge fence that surrounded the yard, so enthralled was he by her beauty, and he leaped over it and landed right next to her. Surely this was why he had traveled so far! Surely this was why he had searched!

At once he kissed her and at once the curse was off!

Sleeping Doggy was so excited, she began to do tricks for King. She shook hands, sat up, rolled over. She even did a card trick for him, which he didn't altogether understand, but wagged his tail at it nevertheless.

The mean old dog heard of Sleeping Doggy's rescue and subsequent happiness, and of course became cranky, really cranky. She was last seen trying to crash an obedience school graduation on the Lower East Side.

King, being enterprising as well as adventurous, decided to put Sleeping Doggy on the road. One of these days when she gets all of her tricks out of her system, they will settle down and live happily ever after. However, they are currently billed as "King and his *Amazing Doggy* Act" — because now that is what she is.

Roi Hide
CHEW STRIPS

"THE KING OF
DOGGY TREATS"
-Charlie Mange

Golden
Nugget
KIBBLE

The official
kibble of King
Arfer's Round Table.

King Muttas and the Golden Touch

NCE UPON A TIME, there lived a mutt who was fortunate enough to be king. His name was King Muttas.

Poor King Muttas. Somewhere along the way he became confused and ended up with a warped sense of values for a dog.

King Muttas was not interested in dogfood or dogbones. He was not interested in savory gravies or little rubber dogtoys. Alas! He was only interested in gold.

Once when he was randomly perking his ears, he overheard a person say that gold was indeed very valuable. King Muttas had not hung around to hear the person say, "...but not for a dog!" He was so overcome by a sudden craving for gold that he started digging up every yard in the country. Poor King Muttas. Try as he did, he could not lay his paws on any.

One day what should appear at the dogcastle door but a weird little dog with a little pointy tail, little pointy ears, and strange little pointy paws. But for the fact that he was green, he resembled a pointer.

"King Muttas, " barked the weird little green dog. "Come to your door, for I am the elf dog of the woods, and I am here to grant you one wish."

"BowWOW!" barked King Muttas. "But why me? I do not recall sending away for a wish." Nevertheless King Muttas grinned in a way only greedy mutts can grin.

"You are the winner of our Annual Dog Day Raffle. A well-meaning dog sent your name in. Now start barking, for I must grant you your wish before sundown."

King Muttas pondered for a moment. Actually he only feigned pondering for the elf dog's benefit, as he did not want to appear greedy. Then he barked:

"I wish that everything I touched would turn to GOLD!"

"You sure about that, King?" barked the elf dog. "Sure you don't wish everything you touch would turn to ham, roast beef, or ground round?"

"GOLD, I want GOLD!" barked King Muttas once again. He was becoming very excited.

"Oooookay!" yipped the elf dog. Then he disappeared.

59

King Muttas looked at his paws. They certainly looked no different. Despite this, he decided to try out his newly granted wish. He touched the gate of his dogcastle.

"GOLD!!!!" he howled. "Eureka!" he barked. And leaping and jumping, he bounded from tree to tree, birdbath to birdbath, gazebo to gazebo until everything in his courtyard was solid gold.

King Muttas looked around, quite pleased with his rapidly increasing wealth of gold. True, he did not know *why* he liked gold *so* much, but he heard that it was valuable, so he figured deep in his heart that he *must* like it.

Woe to King Muttas. Soon enough he heard the bell ring and began salivating. It was dinnertime. He bounded over to his dish on the kitchen floor and dived into the mound of dogfood. CLINK! Solid-gold nuggets greeted him. Then he chomped down on a large meaty bone. CLUNK! The cold yellow metal rattled his canines. Then he went to his water dish in order to wash

down some of the tasteless gold flakes. CLONK! Solid gold water in a solid gold dish. Woe to King Muttas!

He leaped to his paws, dashed over to the phone, and barked into the receiver:

"Get me the elf dog's doghouse!" Which the operator did.

"WOOF! Elf dog's doghouse. . . ."

"WOOF! Listen. This is King Muttas, king of all the

land. You've got to hightail it back here and take this wish away. I am the wealthiest dog on earth but I am starving to death! I wish I'd never made that silly wish!"

"Sorry, King. If wishes were horses — "

"If wishes were horses, doggies would eat! But this golden-touch thing is going to starve me to death!"

"If you want, I can sell you a raffle ticket for next year's Annual Dog Day Raffle."

"You will sell them to a pile of dog's bones then," whimpered King Muttas. "I shall surely starve to death by then."

"Sorry."

"Aughhh!" growled King Muttas for he was most upset. "I must find a way to save myself," he barked.

All of a sudden a thought came!

"I shall issue a DECREE!" King Muttas barked, and at once he began walking in circles and wagging his tail, something he did when he was especially happy.

The following day King Muttas assembled all his subjects together and read them his decree:

"Henceforth, beginning this first warm day of summer, there will be not one, but *many* Annual Dog Days...." All of the doggies clapped their paws and barked "YAY!" "...however, you must all lie down and act lazy, and if the elf dog shows up selling raffle tickets, you must all pretend to be asleep."

All of the doggies barked "BOO!" which made a racket, but King Muttas left them to their disappointment and he bought up all the raffle tickets.

As luck would have it, sometime near the end of the summer, King Muttas won the Dog Day Raffle and wished away his golden touch.

Unfortunately he forgot to un-issue his decree and it is still rather obvious. The world's dogs are too busy lying around and acting lazy during all the Dog Days to do anything about it though.